5-Minute Minute Disney Junior Stories

DISNEY PRESS
Los Angeles • New York

First Hardcover Edition, February 2015   10 9 8 7 6 5 4 3 2 1

ISBN 978-1-4847-1327-3

Library of Congress Control Number: 2014947839

G942-9090-6-14353

Printed in the United States of America

For more Disney Press fun, visit www.disneybooks.com

CONTENTS

Once Upon a Princess

In a small village, in the kingdom of Enchancia, lives a little girl named Sofia. She often helps out her mother, Miranda, who works as a cobbler. One morning, Sofia and her mother go to the castle to bring King Roland a new pair of shoes. He and Miranda take one look at each other, and it's love at first sight.

The couple soon marries, and Sofia and Miranda move into the castle with the king and his two children, Amber and James. To welcome Sofia into the family, King Roland plans a royal ball in her honor. He also gives her a beautiful gift.

"It's a very special amulet," the king explains, "so you must promise to never take it off."

Sofia hugs the king and queen good night and runs toward her room with a big smile on her face.

In the hallway, Cedric stops in his tracks. The king's royal sorcerer immediately recognizes Sofia's necklace. It's the Amulet of Avalor—the powerful pendant Cedric has been trying to get for years! With its magic, Cedric could rule all of Enchancia. Now Cedric just needs to come up with a plan to get the amulet.

The next morning, Sofia starts her first day at Royal Prep Academy. The other students like her a lot, which makes her stepsister, Amber, feel a little jealous. So Amber convinces Sofia to take a ride on the magic swing at recess. It's fun at first, but then the swing speeds up and sends Sofia flying into the fountain!

James feels terrible for not stopping Amber's trick.

Holding back her tears, Sofia runs from the playground and into the woods to dry off her dress. There she finds a baby bird that has fallen out of its nest. As she gently places the bird back in the nest with its mother, the amulet around her neck begins to glow.

When she turns to leave, she thinks she hears a tiny, squeaky voice say "thank you." But birds can't talk . . . can they?

The next morning, Sofia is greeted by Clover the rabbit, Whatnaught the squirrel, and their bird friends, Robin and Mia. They've come to help her get ready for school—and Sofia can understand every word they're saying! She can't believe her ears.

Then Sofia remembers something. "When I helped the baby bird yesterday, I think the amulet gave me the power to understand and talk to animals!"

Later that day, Amber plays another mean trick on her new stepsister. Knowing that Sofia is nervous about dancing in front of everyone at the ball, she gives Sofia a pair of trick shoes during dance class. They make her spin and twirl helplessly out of control.

Afraid there might be another dance disaster at the ball, Sofia asks Cedric for help. "I have just the spell for you," the sorcerer says, showing Sofia some magic words to say when the waltz begins. Little does she know that the spell will put everyone to sleep and help Cedric steal the amulet!

James storms into Amber's room as she gets ready for the ball.

"You gave Sofia the trick shoes on purpose," he says angrily. "You're trying to ruin her ball, because everyone likes her more than you. And after what you did today, so do I!"

"James! Wait!" Amber chases after James—and accidentally tears her gown!

How can she go to the ball now?

At the ball,
everyone watches as
King Roland proudly
escorts Sofia into the
ballroom. The orchestra begins to play. It's time for the
first waltz!

Sofia confidently says the magic words Cedric gave her:
"Somnibus populi cella."

Everyone instantly falls asleep—including Cedric!

"Oh, no! What have I done?" Sofia cries, running out of the room. A single tear falls onto her amulet and makes it glow. Suddenly, a blue light appears—and transforms into Cinderella!

"Your amulet brought me here," Cinderella explains. "It links all the princesses that ever were. And when one of us is in trouble, another will come to help.

"Sofia, I can't undo the spell, but I know you'll find the answer you need." Cinderella suggests that Sofia try to become true sisters with Amber—something she'd never been able to do with her own stepsisters. "Perhaps all she needs is a second chance." Then Cinderella disappears!

Sofia finds Amber and brings her to the ballroom. Amber gasps when she sees everyone under the sleeping spell.

Sofia feels terrible. "It's all my fault!"

Amber shakes her head. "No, Sofia, you wouldn't have needed the spell if I didn't give you those trick shoes."

The girls realize that what they really needed all along was each other.

The sisters rush to Cedric's workshop in search of a spell to wake everyone up. Clover tricks Cedric's pet raven, Wormwood, into revealing where Cedric's counterspell book is hidden. The raven doesn't realize that, thanks to her amulet, Sofia can understand every word he says!

As the girls head back to the ballroom, Amber looks down at her torn dress. "I can't go in there looking like this."

But Sofia isn't about to leave her sister behind. She quickly grabs a needle and thread and mends the gown. "There you go— good as new!"

Now it's Amber's turn to help. She takes Sofia's hand and shows her sister how to waltz properly.

Sofia smiles as she takes her place beside the king. *"Populi cella excitate!"* To her relief, everyone wakes up.

"Uh-oh!" Cedric says when he realizes his plan didn't work. Then he flicks his wand and disappears in a puff of smoke.

King Roland and Sofia begin to waltz.

Sofia looks up at her new dad. "I've been wondering, why do they call you Roland the Second?"

The king explains that his father was also named Roland. Sofia giggles. "So I guess that makes me Sofia the First!"

And it's plain to see that this princess is going to live happily ever after!

Dark Knight

"Who's ready for our big sleepover party?" asks Doc.

"We are!" Lambie, Hallie, Stuffy, and Chilly shout together.

"What are we going to do at the party, Doc?" asks Chilly.

"Well, we're going to play games, tell stories . . ."

"And have a pajama fashion show?" wonders Lambie.

"Sure," giggles Doc. "And I have a special surprise guest!"

"'Tis I, Sir Kirby! The bravest knight in all of McStuffins Kingdom," Sir Kirby announces as he bursts out of the toy castle to greet his friends.

The toys all cheer, and Sir Kirby bows in appreciation.

"We're so glad Donny is letting you sleep over tonight," says Doc. "It's going to be so much fun."

Sir Kirby smiles. "I am most delighted to be here, friends, as it is my first sleepover party ever."

"Oh, you'll love it, sugar!" says Hallie. "We're going to play all sorts of exciting games and get all snuggly in our sleeping bags."

"And then we'll turn off the lights and tell silly stories!" adds Stuffy. "Won't that be fun?"

Sir Kirby starts looking around the room nervously.

"Uh, excuse me, did you say you'd be turning *off* the lights?"

"Yes, why?" asks Doc.

Doc notices a sudden change in Kirby. He doesn't seem to
be acting like himself. "Sir Kirby, you're breathing really hard.
Are you okay?"

"Oh, yes . . . yes! I'm perfectly fine," Kirby answers quickly.
"Being brave is just so . . . uh, tiring."

"Well, I know something we can all do that's not tiring at all,"
Lambie suggests. "In fact, it's really exciting! Let's play party games!"

First the gang builds a
tower of blocks . . .

. . . then it's time for the
sleeping bag hopping race . . .

. . . and, finally, the slumber party fashion show!

The friends laugh and play late into the night. They all agree
that this is the best sleepover party ever!

Doc yawns. "Okay, everyone, it's time to snuggle up and turn off the lights."

But as she walks toward the lamp on her bedside table, Sir Kirby dashes across the floor, jumps up on the table, and blocks the front of the lamp.

"My lady," cries Sir Kirby, "I must ask you not to turn off that light."

Doc is confused. "Well, why not?"

Sir Kirby struggles for an answer. "Well, you see, uh . . . I haven't done my nightly check of the room. It's one of my most important knightly duties." He hops off the table and stops at the edge of Doc's bed to make sure the coast is clear. "I need to make sure there are no monsters here. After all, I do need to keep fair Princess Lambie and Madame Hallie safe."

When the lights accidentally get switched off, Sir Kirby screeches at the top of his lungs!

"*Yiiiiiiiiiiiiiikes!*"

Doc turns the lights back on and sees Sir Kirby shivering in Lambie's arms. "Is everything okay?" she asks.

Sir Kirby pretends he's not nervous. "Why, of course! I was just . . . uh, just keeping Princess Lambie safe from any mean ogres."

"Hmmm . . . breathing heavy, fast heartbeat, and shaky and sweaty when the lights go off," notes Doc. "I have a diagnosis! You, Sir, have a bad case of the Dark Willies. It means you're afraid of the dark!"

"But, Lady McStuffins, how can I be a brave knight if I'm afraid?" asks Sir Kirby.

"Everyone's afraid of something, even brave knights," Doc assures Sir Kirby. "I'm afraid of thunder and lightning."

"I'm afraid of hurting people's feelings," says Lambie, "and of polka dots. I do NOT like polka dots!"

"I'm afraid of getting too hot, getting too cold, melting, getting lost under the bed, being mistaken for a dog toy, being mistaken for a baby toy, and bananas . . . oh, and pickles!" announces Chilly.

"Well, I'm not afraid of anything . . . er, except spiders!" admits Stuffy.

"To treat you, I need to know exactly what caused your Dark Willies," says Doc.

Sir Kirby thinks about it and points toward Doc's rocking chair, which has Doc's jacket hanging from it. "When darkness fell, I saw something strange over there—like a scary monster!"

Doc, Lambie, and Stuffy inspect the rocking chair. "Nothing scary over here," Stuffy reports.

"Maybe this chair looks different in the dark," suggests Doc. "Sir Kirby, will you be okay if we turn off the lights for just a second?"

Sir Kirby sighs. "If you must."

"Here, I'll hold your hand so you won't be scared," offers Lambie.

Chilly chimes in. "Me too!"

Doc prepares Sir Kirby. "Okay, get ready: I'm shutting off the lights on the count of three!"

When the lights go out, Kirby looks toward the rocking chair.

"*Aaack!*" screams Sir Kirby. "Over there—it's the scary monster!"

Doc quickly switches on her flashlight. "No, it's not a monster—it's just the way the jacket looks on the chair when the lights are out. Nothing to be afraid of here!"

"By Jove, you're right!" says Sir Kirby.

Doc thinks she has a cure for Sir Kirby's Dark Willies. "Let's use a night-light for our sleepover, so it won't be so dark when we turn the lights out."

"I'm ready to give it the royal try!" agrees Sir Kirby.

With the night-light on, Sir Kirby feels much safer. "A hundred thanks to you all! Friends, toys, countrymen: Sir Kirby is back and ready for a sleepover party!"

The friends all cheer.

With the Dark Willies gone, the friends are ready to tell
bedtime stories. But as soon as he gets into his sleeping bag,
Sir Kirby falls fast asleep.

"Looks like the good knight just needed a night-light to say
good night!" Lambie says softly.

Doc nods and whispers, "Nighty-night, brave knight!"

The Buttercups

Sofia and her best friends, Ruby and Jade, are excited for their weekly Buttercup meeting.

"Gather round, girls," calls Mrs. Hanshaw, Ruby's mom and the troop's leader. "Meet our newest members, Peg and Meg!"

The scouts welcome the twins to the group and present them with their official Buttercup vests.

"You're Buttercups now!" cheers Sofia.

Jade explains to Peg that Buttercups can earn special badges. "For every new activity you do—like swimming, bird calling, or fort building—you earn a badge for your vest."

"When a Buttercup's vest is filled with badges, she receives a special sunflower pin," continues Mrs. Hanshaw.

Meg glances at Sofia's vest. "Sofia, it looks like your vest is almost full!"

Mrs. Hanshaw smiles. "Yes, Sofia only needs one more badge to get her pin. Tomorrow is her big chance—we'll be going on a hike through Peppertree Forest."

Sofia can't wait to earn her sunflower pin, but King Roland is worried. "What if something happens to you?" he asks. "What if you fall? I can't let you go alone. Baileywick, I'd like you to accompany the princess."

"Dad, I'll be fine on my own," Sofia pleads.

But King Roland's mind is made up.

"Don't worry, Princess," Baileywick assures her, "you'll barely notice I'm there."

The next morning, Sofia puts on her Buttercup uniform and packs a small backpack.

"It's a perfect day for a hike," says Mom.

"It sure is!" Sofia agrees.

Just then, Baileywick appears in the front hall dressed in a Groundhog uniform and carrying an enormous backpack.

"A Groundhog is always prepared!" he says, laughing.

Miranda gives Sofia a kiss good-bye. "Don't worry, everything will be just fine."

As the girls hike through the forest, Baileywick stays close to Sofia. He holds a parasol to shade the princess from the sun.

He trims branches to clear the way for her.

He sweeps the path in front of her so she won't get dirty.

Baileywick pulls out a foldable throne when she wants to sit.

He even pours her a drink in a fancy royal goblet and serves it on a silver tray.

Sofia wishes Baileywick would stop fussing over her. She just wants to hike like the other Buttercups!

It's time for the troop to earn their birdhouse badges. Sofia can't wait! She scurries behind a bush to start gathering twigs for the project.

Baileywick chases after her. "I'll take the twigs—you might get a scratch."

Baileywick pulls out a toolbox from his backpack and starts building a birdhouse.

"I can do it myself," Sofia tells him. But Baileywick just keeps working.

The girls present their finished birdhouses to Mrs. Hanshaw.

Ruby and Jade get badges for their bark- and moss-covered birdhouses.

"Well, that is impressive," Mrs. Hanshaw says when she sees Baileywick's bird mansion. "But to earn a badge, Sofia, you have to do the project yourself."

"I know," sighs Sofia.

Sofia is excited, because she has another chance to earn a badge. This time it's for gathering wood in the forest.

"No splinters for you, Princess," chirps Baileywick. "I'll gather your wood in no time!"

"Baileywick, wait!" pleads Sofia.

But Baileywick doesn't listen. He picks up every log, branch, and twig in sight.

"Time's up, Buttercups!" calls Mrs. Hanshaw.

Baileywick holds up Sofia's pile of logs. All the other girls gathered their own wood.

"I'm sorry, Baileywick, but it only counts if Sofia does it by herself," Mrs. Hanshaw patiently reminds him.

Everyone gets a badge except for Sofia.

At lunchtime, the Buttercups build a campfire and start roasting hot dogs.

When Baileywick begins to roast a hot dog for Sofia, she speaks up.

"Baileywick, I can do all of these tasks myself," she says. "And if I don't, I won't earn my sunflower pin."

Baileywick realizes that Sofia is right. He promises to leave her alone.

After lunch, the Buttercups hike uphill to a meadow. It's
Sofia's last chance to earn a badge.

Mrs. Hanshaw holds up a book about plants. "Everyone must
pick a bouquet of daisies and daffodils, but be careful not to
touch this red flower."

"Why is that?" asks Peg.

"It's Meddlesome Myrtle," replies Mrs. Hanshaw. "If you
touch it, you can get an itchy rash."

Sofia skips into the meadow, with Baileywick following close behind her. Not wanting to risk the princess's getting a rash, he grabs a bunch of flowers from the meadow for her.

"Oh, no! What are you doing?" asks Sofia.

"Why, I picked these for you," answers Baileywick.

"But that's Meddlesome Myrtle!" Sofia cries.

A red, itchy rash spreads over Baileywick's skin, and his cheeks start to puff up! He needs to see a doctor right away, but he can't walk down the trail.

Sofia has an idea. "Let's build a sled with the wood we've collected! That way, we can slide down the hill and get help."

Sofia leads the troop in the project, fastening the sled together with vines and then handing out helmets from Baileywick's backpack.

Everyone jumps on the finished sled, and they ride it all the way back to the castle.

With the castle doctor's help, Baileywick is soon feeling better. King Roland thanks him for watching out for Sofia.

"She didn't need me at all—I was the one who needed *her* help!" Baileywick admits. "She's a great leader, just like you."

Mrs. Hanshaw is very proud of Sofia. She tells Queen
Miranda about how Sofia's quick thinking helped save the day.

"Sofia, you are a true leader," says Mrs. Hanshaw. "You've
earned your leadership badge, which means you've also earned
your sunflower pin!"

The Buttercups all cheer for their friend.

The Buttercups have something special for Baileywick, too.

"We'd like to make you an honorary Buttercup troop leader," Sofia announces, helping him into a Buttercup vest.

"I'm honored," says Baileywick.

Then he raises his bandaged arm to recite the official pledge with Sofia: *"Buttercups, Buttercups! Watch us bloom!"*

Minnie's Bow-tique

It's the grand opening of Minnie's Bow-tique! Minnie can't wait for the ribbon-cutting ceremony to officially mark her first day of business. All her friends are excited to celebrate the occasion.

"Oh, my!" says Minnie. "Mickey, I don't have anything to cut the ribbon with!"

"Oh, Toodles!" calls Mickey.

Which Mouseketool can Minnie use to cut the ribbon? Right! The safety scissors. Minnie's Bow-tique is now officially open!

Her friends clap and congratulate her on her new business.

"Welcome to Minnie's Bow-tique, where every bow's unique!" shouts Minnie. "Have fun browsing the shop! At the end of the day, there is going to be a big bow show, so be sure to stick around."

Minnie sells every kind of bow in every style and for any occasion at her Bow-tique!

Clarabelle tries a Grow Bow. When you spritz it with water, it grows and grows! "*Moo*-velous!" marvels Clarabelle.

Daisy likes the Glow Bow. It changes color when your mood changes. She feels happy, so the bow is yellow.

Donald is busy taking pictures with his Photo Bow Tie.

Goofy is making quite the fashion
statement with his El-bow Ties.

Mickey likes the way his
voice sounds through the
speaker of his Microphone
Bow Tie.

And there's even a bow for
Pluto—a Bone Bow Tie!

But Pete is keeping out of sight. He wants a bow, but he's never bought one before. "I'd feel silly if anybody saw me lookin' for a bow," he whispers to himself.

As Pete sneaks away, he accidentally bumps into one of Minnie's displays. Oh, no! There go the bows!

Donald and Mickey help fix the display.

"Thanks for your help," Minnie says after picking up a bow from the floor.

"Aw, phooey," says Donald. "I can't reach the top to put the sign back!"

"Sounds like we need a Mouseketool." Mickey uses his Microphone Bow Tie to call for help: "Oh, Toodles!"

Toodles has building blocks, which Donald uses to make steps. "Ta-da! The display is back to being bow-tastic!" says Donald. "Thanks, Toodles!"

"I'm sure glad they got everything fixed," Pete murmurs from his hiding spot. "I didn't mean to cause trouble. It's just so embarrassin' not knowin' how to shop for bows!"

Pete spies a box on top of the desk he's hiding behind.

"Hmmm, I wonder what kind of bows are in here?" Pete gently lifts the lid of the box, and Butterfly Bows escape!

"Flutterin' flapdoodles!" whimpers Pete. "You Butterfly Bows better get back into your box. Pretty please?"

But the Butterfly Bows flutter away.

"Oh, no! They weren't supposed to come out until the Big Bow Show!" says Minnie.

"We need another Mouseketool," notes Mickey. "Oh, Toodles!"

Goofy chooses Toodles's butterfly net. "I'll catch those flyin' flip-floppers in no time!"

Just then, Minnie spots Pete. "Do you need help, Pete?"

Pete nods. "I want to buy a bow for my aunt Mabel, but I don't know how!"

"Tell me about Aunt Mabel, and I'll help you pick the perfect bow," offers Minnie.

"She's a pizza chef," Pete says proudly.

"Let's see," says Minnie. "If she bakes pizza, I bet she gets pretty hot in her kitchen."

"Hotter than a turtle in flannel pajamas!" agrees Pete.

"Then maybe she'd like this Fan Bow. It will keep her cool and stylish, all at the same time," Minnie says with a smile.

"Ahhh! Cool! Lemme try it," says Pete. He switches the Fan Bow to high.

"Whoa, Nellie!" shrieks Pete. "This Fan Bow sure kicks up a breeze!"

Mickey yells, "Pete, turn it off!"

But by the time Pete figures out how to turn off the Fan Bow, most of Minnie's bows have blown away!

"Oh, no, we've got to get them back in time for the Big Bow Show," Minnie says, worried.

Everyone calls, "Oh, Toodles!"

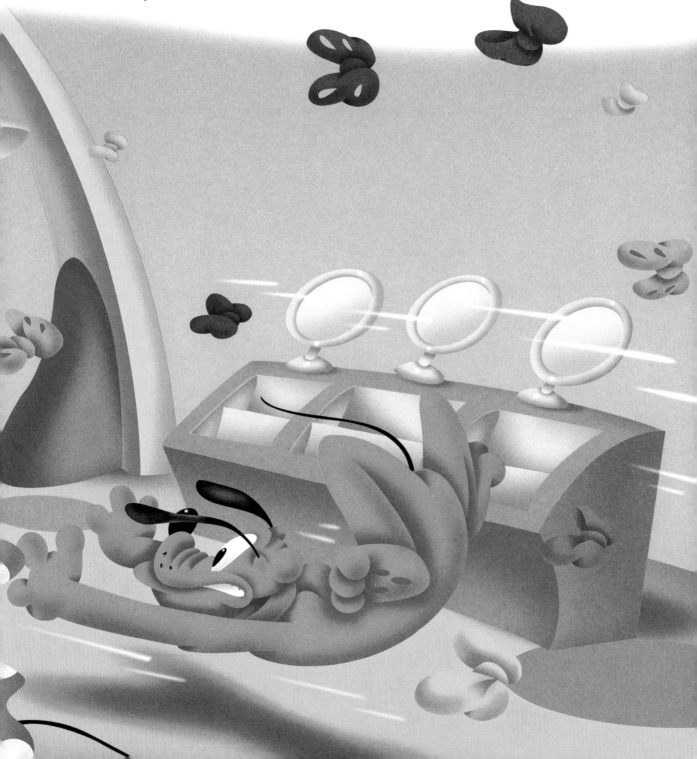

The only Mouseketool left is the Mystery Mouseketool. It's Coco the monkey!

"Great," says Minnie. "She can climb up into the tree and toss the bows down to us."

Soon Donald is covered in bows. "I think she's monkeying around with me," he says.

Minnie catches the last bow. Super cheers!

Now it's time for the best part of the grand opening of Minnie's Bow-tique: the Big Bow Show! Minnie and her friends dazzle on the runway, showcasing their sparkly and spectacular collection of bows.

Mickey, Donald, and the rest of the crowd give Minnie's Bow Show a huge round of applause.

"Now that's what I call a bow-rific show!" says Mickey.

Doctoring the Doc

It's time for Doc McStuffins to open her clinic, but she isn't feeling quite like herself. Doc's friends are inside waiting for her.

"Hi, Doc!" exclaims Lambie.

"Glad you're here, sugar!" says Hallie.

Doc greets them more quietly than usual. "Hi, guys," she says.

Lambie and Stuffy can't wait to play and spend the day with Doc.

But Chilly isn't feeling so great. "Can you feel my belly? It's all lumpy."

"Come on, let's take a look," Doc answers, escorting Chilly to the checkup room.

Lambie notices that Doc seems a bit tired. "Is she okay?"

"She does seem a little draggy and saggy," notes Hallie.

"Hallie, could I have the tweezers so I can look in Chilly's ears?" Doc says. Then she laughs. "Wait—what? Did I say 'tweezers'? I didn't mean the tweezers."

Hallie is surprised. Doc never gets the instruments mixed up!

"Okay, I'm ready to give your diag—*achoo!* Your diagno—*achoo!*" Doc sneezes twice more before continuing. "Chilly, you have Stuffed-Belly-itis. It means your belly is filled with stuffing, just like it should be. You're fine!"

"Chilly may be fine, but I'm not sure you are, Doc," Hallie says gently.

Doc realizes she's right. "I guess . . . I'm not feeling so good."

"You've always taken care of us, Doc," says Stuffy. "Now we're gonna take care of you."

"It's time for *your* checkup!" announces Chilly.

Lambie gives Doc a loving pat. "Now don't be scared, Doc. We're here to help you. And if you need a cuddle, they're free for the asking."

Hallie listens to Doc's heartbeat and then touches her forehead. "You're feeling a little warm to me."

Doc sniffles, so Lambie hands her a tissue. "And your nose is running."

After Stuffy checks her eyes and ears, he has a diagnosis. "Doc, you have a severe case of Leaky-Sniffle-itis."

Hallie wishes they could help Doc, but they only know how to help fix toys. "I think you need a doctor."

Luckily, they don't have to go far to find one. Doc's mom is
a doctor!

The toys pile into the wagon to follow their friend inside. Doc finds her mom in the kitchen. "Mom, I'm not feeling well. My throat kinda hurts, I'm sneezing a lot, and I've got the sniffles. I just feel blah!"

"Let's head to my office for a checkup," Mom says.

First Mom inspects Doc's throat. "Open up!" Next she checks Doc's eyes and ears. Then it's time to take Doc's temperature.

"Sweetie, you have a slight fever, but you'll feel better if you drink lots of liquids and get some rest. Doctor's orders!"

Mom gives Doc a kiss on the head and sends her to bed. "Today is officially a sick day."

Doc scoops up her toys and heads upstairs. Her friends promise to take good care of her.

Hallie blows a whistle. "Troops, we've got a VIP patient in need of our help! Doc, you're gonna lie down! Squeakers, fluff that pillow! Lambie and Stuffy, tuck her in tight!"

"Can't move . . . need to sneeze!" says Doc.

Quickly, the toys pull the covers free so Doc can grab a tissue. *"Achooo!"*

Chilly turns on the radio. "How about a little music?"

"And a get-well dance?" adds Lambie.

"Turn it down!" Hallie blows her whistle again.

Then Stuffy tries to bring Doc a glass of water, but he trips over a block! Doc hops out of bed just in time to catch the glass.

Then, to help her rest, Stuffy and Lambie tell Doc a story about a dragon and a princess on an island. Lambie spins the globe to show Doc the island, but Stuffy's tail gets caught in it.

Lambie tries to help. "Hold still. I'll pull!"

Before they know it, they both tumble off the desk. "Help!" cries Lambie.

"Double help!" yelps Stuffy.

Doc jumps out of bed again to rescue her friends.

"No, you need to be resting!" Hallie shouts.

When Mom hears all the commotion in Doc's room, she pops in. "Doc, what are you doing out of bed?"

Doc is startled. "Oh, I . . . uh . . . I had to save my toys?"

Mom tucks Doc back into bed. "You're sick, and the best way for your body to get better is for you to rest—*really* rest."

After her mom leaves, Doc tells her friends that she really needs some quiet so she can fall asleep.

"Well, there's one thing we can do better than anyone else can to help you rest," says Lambie. "We can let you cuddle with us while you sleep!"

The toys climb into bed with Doc and snuggle close, and Doc and her friends fall fast asleep.

The next morning, the toys wake up before Doc.

Hallie touches Doc's forehead and smiles. "Cool as a cucumber."

Doc opens her eyes and sits up. "Morning, everyone! I'm feeling a lot better. Thanks for letting me rest."

Lambie giggles. "A good night's sleep is just what the doctor ordered!"

"Morning, sweet pea," says Doc's mom, coming into the room. She feels Doc's forehead. "Your fever's gone."

"I feel much better," Doc says. "I had the best care ever."

Mom smiles, thinking Doc means the care she had given her. She doesn't know that Doc is talking about her toys, too!

"Do you think I can go outside and play?" asks Doc.

Mom thinks for a minute before answering. Doc doesn't have a fever anymore. Her sneezing has stopped—and she seems to have a lot more energy. "Well, as long as you take it easy for a day or so, I don't see why not," Mom says.

Back at the clinic, the toys scramble to help Doc.

"Do you want to sit down for a spell, sugar?" asks Hallie.

"Maybe you need an ice pack," Chilly suggests.

"How about some extra cuddles? I'm worried you didn't get enough!" says Lambie.

"Let me take your bag," offers Stuffy. "Whooooa, it's heavy!"

Doc smiles. "Guys, I rested and I'm feeling much better, really. No need to fuss over me."

The friends are relieved to have Doc back in the clinic.

"I'm glad you're feeling better, because I'm pretty sure my Stuffed-Belly-itis is back!" groans Chilly.

Doc laughs. "Well, I couldn't have done it without my wonderful team of doctors. They were the best medicine! Now let's get to that checkup, Chilly. The Doc is back in!"

Just One of the Princes

The trumpet sounds, and the crowd cheers. It's the start of the Flying Derby Race!

Sofia is thrilled to watch the race with her family. "Wow, I wish I could ride through the air like that."

"Royal Prep has its own flying derby team," her brother, James, tells her. "In fact, we have our first practice tomorrow."

The next day, Sofia visits the Royal Prep stables to talk with
Sir Gilliam, the team's coach.

"Why, hello, Princess," he says. "The bleachers are over there,
if you'd like to watch us practice."

"Oh, I didn't come to watch, Sir Gilliam," says Sofia. "I came
to try out for the team!"

Prince Hugo and the other boys start to laugh. They can't believe their ears. "Only princes can ride in the derby," says Hugo.

Amber pulls her aside. "I'm sorry, Sofia, but racing in the flying derby just isn't a princess thing," she explains.

The next day, Sofia returns to the stables to ask the coach for a horse. Sir Gilliam says there's only one horse left in the stable, but nobody wants him.

"I do!" shouts Sofia.

The last flying horse in the stable is named Minimus. He's much smaller than the other racehorses and he seems a bit nervous, but Sofia doesn't mind.

"I think you're perfect!" she says. Minimus gives Sofia a big smile.

"The tryout race is in just a few days," the coach reminds all the riders. "Remember, there are only two spots left on the team, so practice hard!"

The princes climb onto their flying horses. The coach blows his whistle, and the riders take to the sky. Soon they are flying high up with the birds.

But Sofia is still on the ground, trying to climb onto Minimus's saddle. James sees her struggling and flies back down to help her.

"Here, let me give you a hand," James offers.

"Thanks, James." Sofia smiles. "Now what do I do?"

"Flick the reins to take off and then pull them when you want to turn," he explains. "It's easy!"

"Okay, Minimus, let's go!" says Sofia.

Minimus lifts his wings to prepare for takeoff. Sofia tugs on his reins, and before she knows it, they're flying!

Minimus turns his head to give her a big smile.

"Look out!" shouts Sofia when she sees a bird flying straight toward them.

But it's too late. Minimus panics and stops short, causing
Sofia to slip out of her saddle and fall backward.

Poof! Sofia lands on a big soft cushion in the training ring.
James hurries over to make sure she's all right.

"What am I doing wrong?" Sofia asks.

"Listen, Sofia," James says with concern. "We can stop practicing and just go home. . . ."

"I guess racing horses isn't a princess thing after all," says Prince Hugo as he flies past them.

"I'm not giving up!" Sofia says, more determined than ever.

James is proud of his sister. "If you're not giving up, then I won't, either!"

James takes Sofia riding on his own horse to show her how to steer with the reins.

Next she tries riding Minimus. And in no time, she's swooping and zipping through the sky with ease.

"I can fly!" she shouts excitedly.

Finally, James shows Sofia the last leg of the derby course. Racers must fly to the very top of the bell tower to ring the bell.

"Come on, Minimus, I know we can do this," Sofia whispers in her horse's ear. Minimus tries his best, but he's afraid to fly that high. He turns and flies back down to the ground. Sofia can't help feeling disappointed.

Back at the palace, Sofia starts to doubt herself. "Maybe the flying derby *is* just for princes after all."

Queen Miranda reassures her daughter. "Don't give up, Sofia. A princess can do anything a prince can do. Just believe in yourself and keep trying!"

Sofia tries her best and practices every day. At last, the big day arrives: it's time for the tryout race. When the trumpet sounds, the gates open and the horses start flying! The princes are off to a fast start, with Sofia and Minimus trailing behind them.

"We're going to do great, Minimus!" says Sofia encouragingly. "I just know it!"

Sofia expertly guides Minimus over the treetops and under bridges.

The princes cannot believe it. Sofia and Minimus are catching up! Faster and faster they go, flying past every racer until Sofia is in the lead with James just behind her.

But as they near the last hurdle, Minimus gazes up at the bell tower ahead. "We can do this!" Sofia assures her horse.

Minimus is determined to give it everything he has. After all, Sofia believes in him!

"Climb, Minimus! Climb!" shouts Sofia. She and Minimus fly up, up, UP!

They are about to fly through the narrow opening of the bell tower. "Get ready to duck . . . NOW!" And with that command, Sofia rings the bell and Minimus flies through to the other side of the tower. They did it!

The crowd cheers loudly as Sofia and her brother cross the finish line together.

"Princess Sofia and Prince James have made the team!" announces Sir Gilliam. "Congratulations to you both!"

"Good job, Minimus," Sofia says to her friend.

Then, to everyone's surprise, Princess Amber gives Sofia her derby tiara. "I guess I was wrong," she admits with a smile. "Flying derby *is* a princess thing!"

Bronto Bruises

"Pardon me, Miss Lambie, but would you care for a spot of tea?" Doc asks politely.

"A spot of tea would be most lovely, madam!" giggles Lambie. "I say, this is the most divine tea party I've ever attended."

Doc hears running in the hallway. "Uh-oh, sounds like Donny and Mom are home from the arcade. I think you'd better go stuffed!"

"Hey, Doc! Where's Bronty's invitation to the tea party?" jokes Donny.

Doc laughs. "Oh, my, it must've gotten lost in the mail. Bronty is always welcome to join our tea parties."

"You and Bronty can sip tea later," Mom tells Donny. "You're all sticky from lunch at the arcade. It's time for a bath, young man!"

"You can play with Bronty while I'm gone," Donny tells Doc.

When Donny leaves the room, Doc's stethoscope starts to glow and the toys come to life. Bronty gallops around Doc's room.

"Whoa!" giggles Doc. "You sure like to stomp around."

Lambie politely tries to get Bronty's attention. "Would you like to join our tea party?"

"Ooooh, I sure would!" Bronty is so excited that he jumps up on the table, knocking over the teapot and cups.

"Hmmm, maybe tea party isn't the best game for you. Why don't we go outside to play?" Doc suggests.

Bronty is thrilled to play outdoors, where he has enough room to run around. He gallops toward Stuffy, who's holding a ball.

"Ooh, can we play catch? Huh? Can we? Can we? *Puh-leeeeeeze?*" begs Bronty.

Stuffy throws the ball, and Bronty races after it. Chilly and Squeakers have to jump out of his way!

Stuffy throws the ball again, and Bronty runs after it, but he doesn't watch where he's going. He sends Sir Kirby sailing into the air, steps on Ricardo Racecar, and makes Surfer Girl topple to the ground

"Like, careful there, dino dude!" mutters Surfer Girl.

Bronty feels bad. "Oops, sorry."

Surfer Girl tosses the ball, and Bronty runs after it, this time trampling on Stuffy.

"Sorry," Bronty says again. "Now throw it. *Puh-leeeeze?* Throw it, c'mon, throw it!"

Stuffy tosses the ball, but then he decides to take a break from playing. He's feeling a little sore, so he heads into Doc's clinic for a checkup.

Doc listens to Stuffy's heart and lungs with her stethoscope. "Where does it hurt?"

"Well . . . it only hurts here, here, here, here, here, and here," says Stuffy, pointing to his arm, head, foot, stomach, tail, and neck.

"Oh, sweet sugar lumps!" exclaims Hallie. "You've got a whole bushelful of boo-boos!"

Later that night, Sofia tells her animal friends what happened at the stables. "I really want to be on the team, but everyone keeps telling me that it's only for boys," she says sadly.

"That's ridiculous!" grumbles Clover. "If you really want to do it, then you should go for it."

"Oh, you'll love flying," Mia coos. "It's the best feeling in the world!"

Sofia's friends encourage her to try out for the team no matter what anyone says.

"You're right," agrees Sofia. "Anything can be a princess thing!"

"When did the ouches start?" asks Doc.

Stuffy thinks for a moment. "Well, it started when Surfer Girl threw the ball to Bronty, and he jumped up and landed on me."

Doc thinks for a moment and then comes up with a diagnosis. "Stuffy has a severe case of Bronto Boo-Boos. And I have the perfect treatment: a kiss and a cuddle!"

Suddenly, Lambie, Squeakers, Surfer Girl, Sir Kirby, Ricardo, and Star Blazer Zero all come into the waiting room. They all need checkups, too!

Hallie's never seen so many patients in the clinic at once! "Uh-oh, Doc," Hallie says. "I think you have a heaping helping of new patients with Bronto Boo-Boos!"

The toys all line up to get a hug and a kiss from Doc. It's just the medicine they need to feel better!

To make sure the toys don't get Bronto Boo-Boos again, Doc needs to have a talk with Bronty. She finds him standing alone in the backyard.

"Where did everybody go?" asks Bronty. "Are they playing hide-and-seek?"

"No, Bronty, they came to see me at the clinic," Doc begins. Bronty is confused.

"Listen, I know you didn't mean to, but you hurt some of the toys today, and that's why they needed to see me for checkups," Doc says gently.

Bronty can't believe his ears. "*Me?* I-I-I'm sorry, Doc. I didn't mean to hurt anyone. Aww, I hate being so big!"

"Don't say that, Bronty. I like you just the way you are!" says Doc. "Besides, being big is great. You can do so many things that other toys can't do. You just have to be extra careful when you play with smaller toys."

Bronty nods. "Gee, I never thought about that."

"And I have to do the same thing when I play with my little brother, Donny," continues Doc. "I need to remember that I'm bigger than him—I don't want him to get hurt."

Bronty is surprised. "You have to be careful, too? Really?"

"Really! People and toys come in all sizes. You're a big dinosaur—that's who you are and that's terrific! You just can't play so rough."

"Okay, Doc. I'll be careful and won't play rough anymore," Bronty promises.

Bronty finds his friends and apologizes for playing so rough. "I'm sorry, guys. I promise to be extra careful from now on!"

Lambie gives him a big cuddle. "It's okay, Bronty. We still love you!"

Bronty has an idea. "Hey, everyone, do you want to climb on my back and go for a ride around the backyard?"

"Sure, Bronty!" says Stuffy.

Chilly grins. "Sounds like fun!"

The friends giggle and cheer as Bronty gallops around the yard, keeping a gentle, steady pace as he goes.

Doc smiles. "See, Bronty? Being bigger can be pretty cool."

"In a big way!" agrees Bronty.

The Amulet of Avalor

"Tonight we're holding our royal ball, so I have a big surprise for you both!" King Roland announces.

Sofia and Amber follow their dad down a long hallway until they reach a room with gleaming gold doors. It's the castle's Jewel Room, and it's filled with sparkling rings, necklaces, and bracelets.

"You can each pick something to wear to tonight's ball," the king offers. Amber and Sofia shriek with excitement.

That's when a strange creature startles Sofia. It's a griffin— part lion and part eagle.

"Griffins are ideal guards for jewels—they love anything shiny," explains King Roland.

The griffin can't take his eyes off Sofia's amulet. When the girls leave the room with the pretty jewels they picked out, the griffin follows them.

The girls don't realize that the griffin has followed them into Sofia's room. "Let's try on our jewels!" exclaims Amber.

Sofia unclasps her amulet and carefully places it on her nightstand.

While Sofia and Amber are looking at themselves in the mirror, the sneaky griffin grabs the amulet and flies out the window!

After a few minutes, Sofia is anxious
to put her own necklace back on. But
when she returns to the nightstand,
all she sees are marks on the wood.

"My amulet—it's gone!" she cries.

The girls search the room, but with
no luck.

Clover, Mia, and Robin want to help,
but Sofia can't understand them without the amulet!

114

When the girls hear a cry in the dining room, they run downstairs to investigate.

The maid is waving her arms frantically. "I set the golden goblets on the banquet table, and now they're gone!"

Sofia inspects the marks on the table. "Those scratches are just like the ones on my nightstand."

"We must find the thief before the guests arrive for the ball!" states Constable Myers. "I'll call the guards."

Meanwhile, Cedric can't believe his luck: he's just spotted the griffin wearing Sofia's amulet in the Royal Garden!

"Okay, Wormy, I have just the spell to freeze the griffin," Cedric says, cackling. "When I do, you swoop in and grab the amulet. Ready?"

But Cedric casts the spell on the wrong bird!

Cedric unfreezes Wormwood, but it's too late. The griffin flies away.

Cedric is still determined to snatch the amulet from the griffin! So he uses a huge pink diamond to try to lure the griffin into his trap.

"Once the creature goes for the jewel, we'll lower the birdcage on top of him," Cedric explains to Wormwood. "It's a perfect plan!"

Clover, Mia, and Robin spot the griffin inside the castle. He's in the hallway wearing Sofia's amulet *and* Queen Miranda's tiara!

Clover quickly snatches the amulet!

"Gimme that back!" squawks the griffin, gripping the necklace with his sharp talons. "It's mine!"

Clover loses his grip, and the griffin gets away again.

Later, the griffin spies the pink diamond in Cedric's workshop. He flies down and scoops up the jewel. But when Cedric points his wand at the cage to trap the bird, nothing happens.

Cedric lunges at the griffin, determined to snatch the amulet from around his neck, but he's too fast. Cedric gets caught in his own trap.

"Oh, Merlin's mushrooms!" he moans.

Queen Miranda asks the girls if they've seen her missing tiara. There are now scratches and a feather on her dressing table, where the tiara once was.

When Amber tells her parents about the vanishing goblets, she mentions Sofia's missing amulet.

"Your amulet's been stolen, Sofia?" King Roland asks.

Sofia feels terrible and apologizes for breaking her promise always to wear her necklace.

Meanwhile, Cedric chases after the griffin in his homemade
flying machine! The griffin flies so fast that he loses his grip on
the diamond. Next the tiara falls off his head. Cedric catches
them both.

"Geesh, if you're going to drop something, drop the amulet!"
grumbles Cedric.

Suddenly, Cedric's flying machine spins out of control, crashes through the ballroom doors, and skids to a stop. When everyone sees the sorcerer with the diamond and the tiara, they assume he's the thief!

"Cedric, are you the one who's been stealing?" King Roland asks sternly.

Cedric swears he's innocent, but Constable Myers doesn't believe him. "Guards, seize him!" the officer orders.

There must be some way to prove Cedric's innocence, thinks Sofia. She looks down and notices fur and feathers on the floor around Cedric's broken contraption. Then she remembers the scratches that were left at the site of each theft.

"Wait!" Sofia shouts, following the trail of fur and feathers. "Mr. Cedric didn't steal all those things."

Sofia hurries to the banquet table and lifts the tablecloth to reveal the real thief.

Underneath the table, the griffin is playing with his stash of shiny stolen objects—including Sofia's amulet!

Everyone claps for the princess, impressed that she was able to piece together all the clues to solve the mystery! Cedric is relieved, too. He even thanks Sofia for proving he wasn't the thief.

King Roland scoops up the griffin. "It's time for you to find your way back to the Jewel Room, where you belong, little one," says the king with a laugh. He tickles the griffin's chin.

"That tickles!" the griffin says, giggling.

When Sofia hears what the griffin says, she realizes that now that she has her amulet back, she can talk to her animal friends again!

Sofia excuses herself and runs into the hall, where Clover, Robin, and Mia are waiting.

"I missed you all so much!" she cries as they happily gather around her.

"I don't know what we'd do without you," says Clover.

Sofia smiles and decides her friends' voices are the sweetest things she's ever heard!

Minnie's Pet Salon

Today is the day of Pluto's All-Star Pet Show! All the Clubhouse pets will be onstage, but only one will win the prize for Best in Show.

"Minnie's Pet Salon is open for business!" Minnie announces. "We have everything here to make your furry friends look fabulously pet-tastic for the show."

The gang brings their pets to the salon. Goofy brings his kitty, Mr. Pettibone; and his frog, Fiona. Daisy drops off her bunny, Captain Jumps-a-Lot. Clarabelle brings Bella the puppy; Pete is right behind her with Butch the bulldog; and Donald shows Boo-Boo Chicken the way to the salon.

"So many pets!" gasps Minnie. "I might need a little help from my friends."

Daisy helps with the Dog and Cat
Wash. She and Pluto are ready to give
Bella a bath. Daisy fills the tub with
warm water and accidentally pours in
too much bath soap.

The pink bubbles grow and grow! Daisy
jumps into the tub to find Bella and is soon covered in bubbles.
No matter what she does, she can't seem to shake them off.
Minnie comes to the rescue, calling for Toodles.

Toodles has four Mouseketools: a jar of fireflies, a towel, a baby elephant, and a Mystery Mouseketool.

Minnie has a bright idea. "The baby elephant can fill his trunk with water and then rinse the bubbles off of Daisy and Bella!"

Minnie's plan works!

"Yay!" cries Daisy. "Now Bella is ready for Pluto's pet show."

At the Beauty Bar, Donald is trying to put bows on Figaro and Mr. Pettibone, but they won't sit still!

The kitties grab ribbons and run around and around Donald. "Aw, phooey," squawks Donald. "It's a *cat*-astrophe!"

Minnie hurries over to help. "A soft blanket might calm the kitties down," she suggests. "Oh, Toodles!"

Toodles has three Mouseketools left. Only one of them is soft like a blanket.

"The beach towel!" shouts Donald. "Let's try that."

Donald holds the soft towel, and Figaro and Mr. Pettibone jump right in. Donald wraps the towel around them, gently tucking them in. The cats close their eyes and start purring.

"What a *purr*-fect solution!" laughs Minnie. With the cats all relaxed and cozy in the towel, Donald and Minnie are able to dress them up in bows.

Next Minnie goes to check on Mickey. He's trying to teach Captain Jumps-a-Lot and Fiona how to jump rope together.

"Maybe they'll do it if we give them a beat," Minnie suggests.

Mickey and Minnie jump rope together and chant, *"One, two, jump when we do! Three, four, jump once more!"*

It works! The bunny and the frog learn how to hop at the same time.

Suddenly, Butch and Bella race by, pulling Goofy behind them. "Whoa! Slow down, doggies!" yells Goofy.

"Goofy needs help!" says Mickey. "Oh, Toodles!"

Mickey selects the Mystery Mouseketool: it's a big sock! "Here, doggies, I have a toy for you!" shouts Mickey.

The dogs stop what they're doing to play tug-of-war with the sock. It works!

As evening falls, it's time for the pet show to begin. Pete and Clarabelle settle into their judges' seats.

"May the best pet win!" declares Judge Clarabelle.

Goofy tries to turn on the lights for the show, but nothing happens! "Gawrsh," says Goofy, frowning, "the lights don't work."

"Oh, dear," Minnie says, worried, "we can't put on a show without lights."

Mickey knows just what to do.

"Oh, Toodles!" he calls once more. Toodles rushes to the stage. He has one more Mouseketool—a jar full of fireflies!

"Ooh, the fireflies can light up the paper lanterns!" cries Minnie. "Great idea, Mickey!"

The stage is lit. The colorful lanterns look beautiful.

"Now it's time for . . . Pluto's All-Star Pet Show!" Mickey announces. Pluto barks and wags his tail.

Donald's pet, Boo-Boo Chicken, kicks off the show with a lively performance. He does a chicken dance while wearing a top hat.

"Way to shake your tail feathers, Boo-Boo!" Donald says proudly.

Next Butch and Bella twirl and leap across the floor in their brightly colored costumes. Everyone cheers for their ballet number.

"Don't forget to *paws* for applause!" Minnie whispers from backstage as they take their bows.

Figaro and Mr. Pettibone have teamed up for an acrobatic routine. Goofy and Minnie hold up hoops for Figaro and Mr. Pettibone to flip and somersault through.

"You're on a roll!" cheers Goofy.

For the finale, Fiona and Captain Jumps-a-Lot dazzle the audience with their synchronized jumping trick.

"You're a hopping success!" Daisy tells the duo.

Everyone claps and cheers as all the performers take a bow. The Clubhouse friends are very proud of their pets. They all did a terrific job! Now it's up to the judges to pick one pet as Best in Show. But Clarabelle and Pete can't decide. They ask Minnie for help.

"We can't agree on the winner, Minnie. We want you to pick the best pet," Pete explains.

"I know what to do," Minnie says with a smile. "All of our pets are the best, so they all win!"

Pete brings the grand prize to the stage. "Pet treats for everyone," he hollers. "Come and get it!"

Mickey and Minnie have a prize for Pluto, too. "It's a medal for putting on the best pet show ever!" says Mickey.

Pluto happily licks Mickey's face. "Hot dog!" giggles Mickey.

Dusty Bear

"Ready or not, here I come!" shouts Doc McStuffins.

Doc is playing hide-and-seek with Lambie and Stuffy. But when Stuffy trips over a pile of boxes in the hall closet, it doesn't take long for Doc to find them.

"Are you two okay?" she asks the stuffed toys.

"We're fine," giggles Lambie.

Doc notices something familiar in one of the boxes. It's a stuffed bear named Teddy B. He used to be her brother's favorite toy! Donny and Teddy B went everywhere together.

"I bet Donny doesn't even know he's here," says Doc. "He'll be so happy to see Teddy B!"

Doc races to her brother's room.
"I found something that's going to
make you very happy," she tells him.

"Wow, I've missed you so much,
Teddy B!" Donny says, giving the bear
a big squeeze. "I have so many things to
show you and lots of new friends for you
to meet!"

But all of a sudden, Donny begins to sneeze. *"Achoo!"*
Then he sneezes again and again. *"Achoo, achoo—ACHOO!"*

Poor Donny can't stop sneezing! Tears start to well in his
eyes, and his nose gets all stuffed up.

Doc is concerned. "Donny, are you okay?"

"I forgot . . . this is why I can't play with him," Donny says glumly. *"Achooooo!"* He holds up the teddy bear.

"Thanks for surprising me, Doc, but—*achooo!*—I think you'd better take Teddy B away."

Doc feels awful for her little brother. She takes the stuffed bear and leaves Donny's room. As soon as she's out the door, Donny stops sneezing!

Doc takes Lambie, Stuffy, and Teddy B to her room. Doc's stethoscope starts to glow, and all the toys come to life.

"I'm so sorry, Teddy B," Doc tells the bear.

"It's okay," he says sadly. "I'm just not Donny's toy anymore."

Doc has an idea. "Teddy B, there's something about you that makes Donny sneeze," she says. "Let's see if we can find out what it is!"

Doc brings Teddy B to her clinic. Hallie, Chilly, and
Squeakers greet him in the waiting room and welcome him.

"Wow, hi, everybody!" Teddy B says with a smile.

Doc explains that Donny had to stop playing with Teddy B.
All the toys huddle around and give him a big hug.

"That's a nice bear hug!" giggles Teddy B.

Doc grabs her doctor's bag. "Okay, Teddy B, it's time for your checkup!"

First Doc listens to his heartbeat and checks his eyes and ears.

"Now I'm going to test your reflexes by gently tapping your knee with my rubber hammer," Doc explains.

As Doc taps Teddy B's knee, a cloud of dust flies up into the air!

Lambie and Stuffy start to cough.

"Wow! That is some dusty, dusty dust," croaks Lambie.

148

Doc has a diagnosis. She draws a picture in her Big Book of Boo-Boos. "Teddy B has a bad case of the Dusty-Musties," she reports.

Teddy B gasps. "What does that mean?"

"It means you're full of dust, and that's what's making Donny sneeze," says Doc. "He has allergies!"

Lambie and Stuffy follow Doc and Teddy B into the house.

On the way, Doc explains her plan to Teddy B. "All we have to do to cure you is to wash off the dust. It's that simple!"

Inside, Doc asks her mom if she'll help wash away Teddy B's Dusty-Musties.

Mom inspects the bear and agrees with Doc's plan.

"I second your diagnosis," she says. "A good wash is just what this bear needs."

Doc and the toys wait by the washing machine while Mom goes to get a fresh bottle of laundry soap.

Teddy B looks at the big washing machine in front of him. He's never been washed before.

"Are you ready for this?" Doc asks him.

"I'll do anything to be Donny's toy again," he replies. "But I have to admit, I'm a little scared."

Lambie and Stuffy want to help Teddy B. They know he's feeling nervous about getting washed. Lambie has an idea.

"What if we go in the washing machine with you?" she suggests.

Stuffy turns to Doc. "Ooh, can we?" he asks.

"Well, you both could certainly use a wash," says Doc, giggling. "That sounds like a great idea!"

When Doc's mom returns with the soap, Doc places the toys in the washer and gently closes the door. Teddy B feels much braver having his new friends come along with him.

"With a little soap and water, these toys will be clean and fresh in no time at all," Mom explains.

She puts laundry soap in the machine and then pushes the start button.

Beep!

Soon the toys are ready. They feel clean and smell great after the wash.

"That was fun!" Teddy B tells Doc. "And look at me—I'm clean! No dust!"

Doc gently taps his knee. "And no more dust clouds! I'm happy to report that you are officially cured of the Dusty-Musties," she says.

"Are you ready to see Donny now?" asks Doc.

"Boy, am I!" shouts the bear.

Doc brings Teddy B outside to see Donny. She tells her brother about the Dusty-Musties.

"But Teddy is cured," she assures Donny. "He won't make you sneeze now!"

Donny gives the bear a hug—and doesn't sneeze. His sister was right!

"Thanks, Doc," he says excitedly. "It's great to have him back again. Come on, Teddy B, let's go play!"

"No more Dusty-Musties for Teddy B!" cheers Lambie.

"Great job, Doc!" adds Stuffy.

"Thanks, guys!" says Doc. "But I couldn't have done it without you."

The Princess Test

One day at Royal Prep, Flora, Fauna, and Merryweather float into Sofia's dance class.

"May I have your attention, please?" asks Flora. "We won't be having dance class today. Instead, you'll be preparing for a very important test."

"The Princess Test!" Merryweather adds.

"It's your chance to show us everything you've learned about being a true princess," explains Fauna.

"Everything?" Princess Jun exclaims. "But we've learned so much!"

The fairies explain that the test will take place in the ballroom right after school. "Good luck, everyone!" Fauna says as the fairies flutter out.

The girls head to the library to prepare for the Princess Test. The librarian, Mrs. Higgins, finds them books to study and wishes them luck.

Sofia starts to worry. "I haven't been a princess very long. There's so much I don't know."

"Just make sure your gown looks gorgeous—like mine—and you'll do fine," Amber assures her. "That's the most important thing to know about being a princess."

Hildegard flips open her fan. "And be sure you know how to properly flutter your fan—that's a must!"

Sofia hopes she can remember everything she's learned so far about being a princess. The Princess Test is about to start!

"You go on without me," Sofia says as the others head for the ballroom. "I want to make sure my dress looks perfect."

The other princesses pass Mrs. Higgins. "Princess Amber!" the librarian calls out. "Can you help me?"

"I wish I could, Mrs. Higgins," Amber replies. "But the Princess Test is about to start."

"I understand, dear," Mrs. Higgins says. She asks Jun and Hildegard for help, but both girls apologize and hurry past as well.

Finally, Sofia comes along. "What's the matter, Mrs. Higgins?" she asks.

"Oh, thank you for stopping!" the librarian cries. "I have to bring these books home, but my wheelbarrow broke and I can't carry them myself. Will you help me? I don't live far—just down the path a wee bit."

"Umm . . ." Sofia glances toward the ballroom, not sure what to do. "Of course!"

Sofia sees that a tree has fallen on the footbridge that leads to Mrs. Higgins's house. "How are we going to get to your cottage?"

"Well, there's another way, but it will take a bit longer."

Sofia gulps. "Longer? But that might make me late for the Princess Test."

"I understand if you need to go back," Mrs. Higgins says.

Sofia thinks about it. Then she shakes her head. "I can't let you carry all these books yourself, Mrs. Higgins. Lead the way."

Soon they come to a narrow path between two boulders.

"After you, my dear!" offers Mrs. Higgins. Sofia steps forward. Then she stops. "I'm so sorry," she says. "A proper princess would say 'after you'!"

Mrs. Higgins smiles. "But you *are* a proper princess."

"Well, I wasn't born a princess," Sofia sighs. "Sometimes I feel like I need to keep proving that I belong."

Mrs. Higgins pats her shoulder. "From what I've seen, Sofia, I think you make a wonderful princess."

After a while, Sofia and Mrs. Higgins come upon a stream. "Where's the bridge?" Sofia asks.

Mrs. Higgins chuckles. "Oh, we don't need a bridge. We can just walk across the rocks."

Sofia hears the school bell in the distance. The Princess Test is starting! She needs to hurry.

Sofia follows Mrs. Higgins over the slippery rocks. While she tries to keep her balance, she drops her fan in the water.

"Wake up, Minnie! Wake up!" call her friends.

"Oh, hello, everybody," Minnie says, yawning. "I must have fallen asleep."

"Thank you for helping us, Minnie," says Daisy. "You finished all the chores."

Mickey holds out a box with a big bow on it. "We have a special surprise for you."

Inside the box, Minnie finds a beautiful pair of glass slippers. "I've dreamed of wearing shoes like these!" she exclaims. "Thank you, everybody!"

Minnie tries on the glass slippers. They fit perfectly!

"You look as pretty as a princess," says Mickey.

"Awww, you're a prince for picking these out for me, Mickey. It's like a dream come true!" Minnie says, giggling. "Come on, everybody, let's have a ball and dance until midnight!"

"Oh, no!" cries Sofia. "Hildegard said the fan is a really important part of the Princess Test. Now I lost it and I'm late. What am I going to do?"

Once again, Mrs. Higgins offers to let Sofia turn back. But Sofia knows the books are too heavy for one person to carry.

"I'm not leaving until we get you home," Sofia insists. "Besides, my gown still looks nice. My sister said that's the most important part of the test."

Mrs. Higgins points ahead. "My cottage is just through those trees. . . ."

To get to the cottage, the two must pass through a muddy bog. Sofia holds up the edge of her gown to keep it clean.

There's just one problem: the mud is slippery. Halfway across the path, Mrs. Higgins slips and falls. Sofia tries to catch her but she falls in the mud, too! Her gown is filthy!

"I'm so sorry, Sofia," Mrs. Higgins says, arriving at her door. "But I couldn't have made it home without you. Thank you!"

Sofia smiles. "You're welcome. I may have missed the Princess Test, but it was worth it."

Mrs. Higgins has a twinkle in her eye. "Don't give up on that test just yet. Come this way. . . ."

Mrs. Higgins leads Sofia into the cottage—which transforms into the Royal Prep ballroom! All the other princesses are inside, along with Flora and Merryweather.

"Sofia!" Amber exclaims. "Where did you come from? And what happened to your dress?"

Sofia is confused—especially when she sees a second Mrs. Higgins standing nearby! The first Mrs. Higgins pulls out a wand and transforms into Fauna.

"I used magic to make myself look like Mrs. Higgins," Fauna explains. "It was all part of the Princess Test! One of the most important things about being a princess is practicing kindness. A true princess always helps a person in need."

The real Mrs. Higgins nods. "Even if it means giving up something very important to you."

Amber and the other princesses all end up doing well on the Princess Test. The fairies reward them with sparkly silver stars.

But Sofia was the only one who stopped to help Mrs. Higgins, so she wins a special gold trophy.

"Can I hold it?" Amber asks eagerly.

"Of course you can," Princess Sofia says with a smile.

Minnie-rella

Mickey and his friends are planning a surprise for Minnie, but they need to keep her busy while they work on it.

"Can you take care of my frog?" Goofy asks.

"And string my ukulele?" says Mickey.

"Could you please sweep the floor, dust the rooms, and fix Pluto's bear?" Daisy requests.

"And wash my rubber duckies?" adds Donald.

"Sure, what are friends for?" Minnie says.

"I've got a lot to do! I'd better get busy," Minnie says.

She starts by washing the rubber duckies. Next she puts new strings on Mickey's ukulele and fixes Pluto's bear.

"I'm so tired," Minnie says, yawning. "But I promised to help my friends. . . ." The teddy bear makes a comfy pillow and soon Minnie is asleep.

"Oh, Minnie-rella!" a voice calls. "I'm your fairy godmother! It's time for you to get ready for Prince Mickey's ball."

"A ball? But I have too much to do!" Minnie-rella frets.

"That's what I'm here for," the Fairy Godmother says, waving her wand. Suddenly, flowers grow out of the floor!

"Oops! Oh, Quoodles!" she calls.

Quoodles arrives with tools. The Handy Helpers help Minnie-rella finish her chores.

"Next you'll need a dress!" The Fairy Godmother waves her wand and a new dress appears, but it's all in pieces.

"Oopsie me," the Fairy Godmother says. "It looks like we may need a little more help." She whistles a happy tune.

Suddenly, cute little creatures fly, dash, and hop into the room.

They sew, zip, button, and tie Minnie-rella's gown together. There's just one thing missing. The Fairy Godmother points to Quoodles.

"What can we use to make a bow?" she asks.

"How about the ribbon?" answers Minnie-rella.

"Good thinking!" says the Fairy Godmother.

With the gown complete, the Fairy Godmother inspects Minnie-rella's shoes. "Oh, my! They won't do at all." She waves her wand.

"Abraca-dabraca-snooze!"
Minnie-rella is wearing slippers!
The Fairy Godmother tries again.

"Abraca-dabraca-swim!"
Now Minnie-rella is wearing flippers!

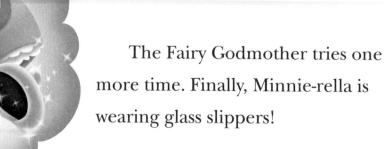

The Fairy Godmother tries one more time. Finally, Minnie-rella is wearing glass slippers!

"Now you're ready to go to the ball!"
the Fairy Godmother announces.

"But how will I get there?"
Minnie-rella wonders.

The Fairy Godmother leads
Minnie-rella to Goofy's garden and asks
Goofy for the biggest pumpkin he has.

"Pumpkins are out of season, but I've got this big tomato,"
Goofy offers.

With a wave of her wand, the Fairy Godmother turns the
tomato into a carriage and Goofy into a coachman! Then she
waves and tells Minnie-rella to be home by midnight.

But the tomato carriage doesn't get too far before its wheel gets stuck in a hole. Minnie-rella calls for Quoodles, who arrives in an instant.

"Let's see," says Minnie-rella. "We have a pillow, Hilda the Hippo, and a mystery tool. Which one can help us push the carriage out of the hole?"

Goofy and Minnie-rella both agree that Hilda is the best choice. She pushes the carriage out of the hole in a flash!

Minnie-rella and Goofy thank Hilda and head to Prince Mickey's castle.

They soon arrive at the castle gate—but they can't get in!

"You need three diamond shapes to unlock the gate," the gatekeeper tells them.

They call for Quoodles, who is happy to help!

Hmmm, Minnie-rella thinks, *we've got a pillow and a mystery tool. Which tool can we use to unlock the gate?*

The pillow is not shaped like a diamond, so they choose the mystery tool instead.

The mystery tool is a bracelet with three diamonds. The gatekeeper uses the three diamond shapes to unlock the gate.

"Right this way, madam," says the gatekeeper politely.

"Have fun at the ball, Minnie-rella!" Goofy says, waving.

"Thanks for the ride," calls Minnie-rella, rushing off to the castle.

As Minnie-rella enters the ballroom, Prince Mickey spots her right away and races to her side. "May I have this dance?"

Minnie-rella curtsies. "Why, yes, Your Majesty!"

The couple glides across the ballroom floor, smiling and laughing.

"Looks like Prince Mickey has found his princess, Pluto," says the Royal Advisor.

The hours fly by until, eventually, the castle clock chimes. It's midnight! "Oh, no!" cries Minnie-rella. "I'm so sorry, but I must go!" she calls, running out of the ballroom.

"Wait!" cries Prince Mickey, chasing after her. But Minnie-rella is already halfway down the castle steps. She must hurry—the spell is about to break!

"I don't even know your name!" Prince Mickey calls. But it's too late. Minnie-rella has already raced through the castle gates and onto the road.

"Gee, how will I ever find her?" asks Prince Mickey.

Pluto barks and points at Minnie-rella's glass slipper.

"To find the mystery princess fast, find the one who fits the slipper made of glass," suggests the Royal Advisor.

The next day, Prince Mickey sets out into the kingdom to find the owner of the glass slipper. Goofy tries it on, but it pops off! Luckily, Quoodles brings the heart-shaped pillow just in time!

Then Goofy remembers that the shoe belongs to Minnie-rella. So he takes Prince Mickey to her. Of course, the glass slipper fits, and the prince and princess live happily ever after!